# THE LIE

—————————

A SHORT STORY

*BY*

# MARY ANTIN

First published in 1918

**British Library Cataloguing-in-Publication Data**
A catalogue record for this book is available
from the British Library

# CONTENTS

———————

# THE MAKING OF A PATRIOT:
## MARY ANTIN

---

*From*
*Heroines of Service by Mary Lyon*
*Published In 1921*

Where is the true man's fatherland?
Is it where he by chance is born?
Doth not the yearning spirit scorn
In such scant borders to be spanned?
O yes! his fatherland must be
As the blue heaven wide and free!

James Russell Lowell.

## THE MAKING OF A PATRIOT

YOU  know the story of "The Man without a Country"—the man who lost his country through his own fault. Can you imagine what it would mean to be a child without a country—to have no flag, no heroes, no true native land to which you belong as you belong to your family, and which in turn belongs to you? How would it seem to grow up without the feeling that you have a big country, a true fatherland to protect your home and your friends; to build schools for you; to give you parks and playgrounds, and clean, beautiful streets; to fight disease and many dangers on land and water for you?—This is the story of a little girl who was born in a land where she had no chance for "life, liberty, and the pursuit of happiness." Far from being a true fatherland, her country was like the cruel stepmother of the old tales.

It was strange that one could be born in a  country and yet have no right to live there! Little Maryashe (or Mashke, as she was called, because she was too tiny a girl for a big-sounding name) soon learned that the Russia where she was born was not her own country. It seemed that the Russians did not love her people, or want them to live in their big land. And yet there they were! Truly it was a strange world.

"Why is Father afraid of the police?" asked little Mashke. "He has done nothing wrong."

"My child, the trouble is that we can do nothing right!" cried her mother, wringing her hands. "Everything is wrong with us. We have no rights, nothing that we dare to call our own."

It seemed that Mashke's people had to live in a special part of the country called the "Pale of Settlement." It was against the law to go outside the Pale no matter how hard it was to make a living where many people of the same manner of life were herded together, no matter how much you longed to try your fortune in a new place. It was not a free land, this Polotzk where she had been born. It was a prison  with iron laws that shut people away from any chance for happy living.

It is hard to live in a cage, be it large or small. Like a wild bird, the free human spirit beats its wings against any bars.

"Why, Mother, why is it that we must not go outside the Pale?" asked Mashke.

"Because the Czar and those others who have the power to make the laws do not love our people; they hate us and all our ways," was the reply.

"But why do they hate us, Mother?" persisted the child with big, earnest eyes.

"Because we are different; because we can never think like

them and be like them. Their big Russia is not yet big enough to give people of another sort a chance to live and be happy in their own way."

Even in crowded Polotzk, though, with police spying on every side, there were happy days. There were the beautiful Friday afternoons when Mashke's father and mother came home early from the store to put off every sign of the work-a-day world and make ready for the Sabbath. The children were allowed to wear their holiday clothes and new shoes. They stepped about happily while their mother hid the great store keys and the money bag under her featherbed, and the grandmother sealed the oven and cleared every trace of work from the kitchen.

How Mashke loved the time of candle prayer! As she looked at the pure flame of her candle the light shone in her face and in her heart. Then she looked at the work-worn faces of her mother and grandmother. All the lines of care and trouble were smoothed away in the soft light. They had escaped from the prison of this unfriendly land with its hard laws and its hateful Pale. They were living in the dim but glorious Past, when their father's fathers had been a free nation in a land of their own.

But Mashke could not escape from the prison in that way. She was young and glad to be alive. Her candle shone for light and life to-day and to-morrow and to-morrow! There were no bars that could shut away her free spirit from the light.

How glad she was for life and sunlight on the peaceful Sabbath afternoons when, holding to her father's hand, she walked beyond the city streets along the riverside to the place where in blossoming orchards birds sang of the joyful life of the air, and where in newly plowed fields peasants sang the song of planting-time and the fruitful earth. Her heart leaped as she felt herself a part of the life that flowed through all things—river, air, earth, trees, birds, and happy, toiling people.

It seemed to Mashke that most of her days were passed in wondering—wondering about the strange world in which she found herself, and its strange ways. Of course she played as the children about her did, with her rag doll and her "jacks" made of the knuckle bones of sheep; and she learned to dance to the most spirited tune that could be coaxed from the teeth of a comb covered with a bit of paper. In winter she loved to climb in the bare sledge, which when not actively engaged in hauling wood could give a wonderful joy-ride to a party of happy youngsters, who cared nothing that their sleigh boasted only straw and burlap in place of cushions and fur robes, and a knotted rope in place of reins with jingling bells.

But always, winter and summer, in season and out of season, Mashke found herself wondering about the meaning of all the things that she saw and heard. She wondered about her hens who gave her eggs and broth, and feathers for her bed, all in exchange for her careless largess of grain. Did they ever feel that the barnyard was a prison? She wondered about the treadmill horse who went round and round to pump water for the public baths. Did he know that he was cheated out of the true life of a horse—work-time in cheerful partnership with man and play-time in the pasture with the fresh turf under his road-weary hoofs? Did the women, who toiled over the selfsame tasks in such a weary round that they looked forward to the change of wash-day at the river where they stood knee-deep in the water to rub and scrub their poor rags, know that they, too, were in a treadmill?—Sometimes she could not sleep for wondering, and would steal from her bed before daybreak to walk through the dewy grass of the yard and watch the blackness turn to soft, dreamy gray. Then the houses seemed like breathing creatures, and all the world was hushed and very sweet. Was there ever such a wonder as the coming of a new day?—As she watched it seemed that her spirit flew beyond the town, beyond the river and the glowing sky itself—touching, knowing, and loving all things. Her spirit was free!

Sometimes it seemed that the wings of her spirit could all but carry her little body up and away. She was indeed such a wee mite that they sometimes called her Mouse and Crumb and Poppy Seed. All of her eager, flaming life was in her questioning eyes and her dark, wayward curls. Because she was small and frail she was spared the hard work that early fell to the lot of her older, stronger sister. So it happened that she had time for her wonderings—time for her spirit to grow and try its wings.

Mashke was still a very little child when she learned a very big truth. She discovered that there were many prisons besides those made by Russian laws; she saw that her people often shut themselves up in prisons of their own making. There were hundreds of laws and observances—ways to wash, to eat, to dress, to work—which seemed to many as sacred as their faith in God. Doubtless the rules which were now only empty forms had once had meaning, such as the law forbidding her people to touch fire on the Sabbath, which came down from a time before matches or tinder-boxes when making a fire was hard work. But all good people observed the letter of the law, and, no matter what the need of mending a fire or a light, would wait for a Gentile helper to come to the rescue.

One memorable evening, however, Mashke saw her father, when he thought himself unobserved, quietly steal over to the table and turn down a troublesome lamp. The gleam of a new light came to the mind of the watching, wondering child at that moment. She began to understand that even her father, who was the wisest man in Polotzk, did many things because he feared to offend the prejudices of their people, just as he did many other things because of fear of the Russian police. There was more than one kind of a prison.

When Mashke was about ten years old a great change came to her life. Her father decided to go on a long journey to a place far from Polotzk and its rules of life, far from Russia and its laws of persecution and death, to a true Promised Land where all people, it was said, no matter what their nation and belief, were free to live and be happy in their own way. The name of this Promised Land was America. Some friendly people—the "emigration society," her father called them—made it possible for him to go try his fortune in the new country. Soon he would make a home there for them all.

At last the wonderful letter came—a long letter, and yet it could not tell the half of his joy in the Promised Land. He had not found riches—no, he had been obliged to borrow the money for the third-class tickets he was sending them—but he had found freedom. Best of all, his children might have the chance to go to school and learn the things that make a free life possible and worth while.

Mashke found that they had suddenly become the most important people in Polotzk. All the neighbors gathered about to see the marvelous tickets that could take a family across the sea. Cousins who had not thought of them for months came with gifts and pleadings for letters from the new world. "Do not forget us when you are so happy and grand," they said.

"You will see my boy, my Möshele," cried a poor mother again and again. "Ask him why he does not write to us these many months. If you do not find him in Boston maybe he will be in Balti-moreh. It is all America."

The day came at last when every stool and feather-bed was sold, and their clothes and all the poor treasures they could carry were wrapped in queer-looking bundles ready to be taken in their arms to the new home. All of Polotzk went to the station to wave gay handkerchiefs and bits of calico and wish them well. They soon found, however, that the way of the emigrant is hard. In order to reach the sea they had to go through Germany to Hamburg, and a fearful journey it proved to be. It was soon evident that the Russians were not the only cruel people in the world; the Germans were just as cruel in strange and unusual ways, and in a strange language.

They put the travelers in prison, for which they had a queer name, of course—"Quarantine," they called it. They drove them like cattle into a most unpleasant place, where their clothes were snatched off, their bodies rubbed with an evil, slippery substance, and their breath taken away by an unexpected shower that suddenly descended on their helpless heads. Their precious bundles, too, were tossed about rudely and steamed and smoked. As the poor victims sat wrapped in clouds of steam waiting for the final agony, their clothes were brought back, steaming like everything else, and somebody cried, "Quick! Quick! or you will lose your train!" It seemed that they were not to be murdered after all, but that this was just the German way of treating people whom they thought capable of carrying diseases about with them.

Then came the sixteen days on the big ship, when Mashke was too ill part of the time even to think about America. But there were better days, when the coming of morning found her near the rail gazing at the path of light that led across the shimmering waves into the heart of the golden sky. That way seemed like her own road ahead into the new life that awaited her.

The golden path really began at a Boston public school. Here Mashke stood in her new  American dress of stiff calico and gave a new American name to the friendly teacher of the primer class. Mary Antin she was called from that day, all superfluous foreign letters being dropped off forever. As her father tried in his broken English to tell the teacher something of his hopes for his children, Mary knew by the look in his eyes that he, too, had a vision of the path of light. The teacher also saw that glowing, consecrated look and in a flash of insight comprehended something of his starved past and the future for which he longed. In his effort to make himself understood he talked with his hands, with his shoulders, with his eyes; beads of perspiration stood out on his earnest brow, and now he dropped back helplessly into Yiddish, now into Russian. "I cannot now learn what the world knows; I must work. But I bring my children—they go to school for me. I am American citizen; I want my children be American citizens."

The first thing was, of course, to make a beginning with the new language. Afterward when Mary Antin was asked to describe the way the teacher had worked with her foreign class she replied with a smile, "I can't vouch for the method, but the six children in my own particular group (ranging in age from six to fifteen—I was then twelve) attacked the see-the-cat and look-at-the-hen pages of our primers with the keenest zest, eager to find how the common world looked, smelled, and tasted in the strange speech, and we learned!" There was a dreadful time over learning to say *the* without making a buzzing sound; even mastering the v's and w's was not so hard as that. It was indeed a proud day for Mary Antin when she could say "We went to the village after water," to her teacher's satisfaction.

How Mary Antin loved the American speech! She had a native gift for language, and gathered the phrases eagerly, lovingly, as one gathers flowers, ever reaching for more and still more. She said the words over and over to herself with shining eyes as the miser counts his gold. Soon she found that she was thinking in the beautiful English way. When she had been only four months at school she wrote a composition on *Snow* that her teacher had printed in a school journal to show this foreign child's wonderful progress in the use of the new tongue. Here is a bit of that composition:

> Now the trees are bare, and no flowers are to see in the fields and gardens (we all know why), and the whole world seems like a-sleep without the happy bird songs which left us till spring. But the snow which drove away all these pretty and happy things, try (as I think) not to make us at all unhappy; they covered up the branches of the trees, the fields, the gardens and houses, and the whole world looks like dressed in a beautiful white—instead of green—dress, with the sky looking down on it with a pale face....

At the middle of the year the child who had entered the primer class in September without a word of English was promoted to the fifth grade. She was indeed a proud girl when she went home with her big geography book making a broad foundation for all the rest of the pile, which she loved to carry back and forth just because it made her happy and proud to be seen in company with books.

"Look at that pale, hollow-chested girl with that load of books," said a kindly passer-by one day. "It is a shame the way children are overworked in school these days."

The child in question, however, would have had no basis for understanding the chance sympathy  had she overheard the words. Her books were her dearest joy. They were indeed in a very real sense her only tangible possessions. All else was as yet "the stuff that dreams are made of." As she walked through the dingy, sordid streets her glorified eyes looked past the glimpses of unlovely life about her into a beautiful world of her own. If she felt any weight from the books she carried it was just a comfortable reminder that this new Mary Antin and the new life of glorious opportunity were real.

When she climbed the two flights of stairs to her wretched tenement her soul was not soiled by the dirt and squalor through which she passed. As she eagerly read, not only her school history but also every book she could find in the public library about the heroes of America, she did not see the moldy paper hanging in shreds from the walls or the grimy bricks of the neighboring factory that shut out the sunlight. Her look was for the things beyond the moment—the things that really mattered. How could the child feel poor and deprived when she knew that the city of Boston was hers!

As she walked every afternoon past the fine, dignified buildings and churches that flanked Copley Square to the imposing granite structure that held all her hero books, she walked as a princess into her palace. Could she not read for herself the inscription at the entrance: Public Library—Built by the People—Free to All—? Now she stood and looked about her and said, "This is real. This all belongs to these wide-awake children, these fine women, these learned men—and to *me*."

Every nook of the library that was open to the public became familiar to her; her eyes studied lovingly every painting and bit of mosaic. She spent hours pondering the vivid pictures by Abbey that tell in color the mystic story of Sir Galahad and the quest of the Holy Grail, and it seemed as if the spirit of all romance was hers. She lingered in the gallery before Sargent's pictures of the "Prophets," and it seemed as if the spirit of all the beautiful Sabbaths of her childhood stirred within her, as echoes of the Hebrew psalms awoke in her memory.

When she went into the vast reading-room she always chose a place at the end where, looking up from her books, she could get the effect of the whole vista of splendid arches and earnest readers. It was in the courtyard, however, that she felt the keenest joy. Here the child born in the prison of the Pale realized to the full the glorious freedom that was hers.

"The courtyard was my sky-roofed chamber of dreams," she said. "Slowly strolling past the endless pillars of the colonnade, the fountain murmured in my ear of all the beautiful things in all the beautiful world. Here I liked to remind myself of Polotzk, the better to bring out the wonder of my life. That I who was brought up to my teens almost without a book should be set down in the midst of all the books that ever were written was a miracle as great as any on record. That an outcast should become a privileged citizen, that a beggar should dwell in a palace—this was a romance more thrilling than poet ever sung. Surely I was rocked in an enchanted cradle."

As Mary Antin's afternoons were made glorious by these visits to the public library, so her nights were lightened by rare half-hours on the South Boston Bridge where it crosses the Old Colony Railroad. As she looked down at the maze of tracks and the winking red and green signal lights, her soul leaped at the thought of the complex world in which she lived and the wonderful way in which it was ordered and controlled by the mind of man. Years afterward in telling about her dreams on the bridge she said:

"Then the blackness below me was split by the fiery eye of a monster engine, his breath enveloped me in blinding clouds, his

14

long body shot by, rattling a hundred claws of steel, and he was gone. So would I be, swift on my rightful business, picking out my proper track from the million that cross it, pausing for no obstacles, sure of my goal."

Can you imagine how the child from Polotzk loved the land that had taken her to itself? As she stood up in school with the other children and saluted the Stars and Stripes, the words she said seemed to come from the depths of her soul: "I pledge allegiance to my flag and to the Republic for which it stands—one nation indivisible, with liberty and justice for all." Those were not words, they were heart throbs. The red of the flag was not just a bright color, it was the courage of heroes; the white was the symbol of truth clear as the sunlight; the blue was the symbol of the wide, free heavens—her spirit's fatherland. The child who had been born in prison, who had repeated at every Passover, "Next year, may we be in Jerusalem," had found all at once her true country, her flag, and her heroes. When the children rose to sing "America," she sang with all the pent-up feeling of starved years of exile:

I love thy rocks and rills,
Thy woods and templed hills.

As the teacher looked into the glorified face of this little alien-citizen she said to herself, "There is the truest patriot of them all!"

Only once as they were singing "Land where my fathers died," the child's voice had faltered and died away. Her cheek paled when at the close of school she came to her teacher with her trouble.

"Oh, teacher," she mourned, "our country's song can't to mean me—*my* fathers didn't die here!"

The friendly teacher, whose understanding and sympathy were never failing, understood now:

"Mary Antin," she said earnestly, looking through the child's great, dark eyes into the depths of her troubled soul, "you have as much right to those words as I or anybody else in America. The Pilgrim Fathers didn't all come here before the Revolution.

15

Isn't your father just like them? Think of it, dear, how he left his home and came to a strange land where he couldn't even speak the language. And didn't he come looking for the same things? He wanted freedom for himself and his family, and a chance for his children to grow up wise and brave. It's the same story over again. Every ship that brings people from Russia and other countries where they are ill-treated is a *Mayflower!*"

These words took root in Mary Antin's heart and grew with her growth. The consciousness that she was in very truth an American glorified her days; it meant freedom from every prison. Seven years after her first appearance in the Boston primer class she entered Barnard College. After two years there and two more at Teachers College, she entered the school of life as a homemaker; her name is now Mary Antin Grabau. Besides caring for her home and her little daughter, she has devoted her gifts as a writer and a lecturer to the service of her country.

In her book, "The Promised Land," she has told the story of her life from the earliest memories of her childhood in Russia to the time when she entered college. It is an absorbing human story, but it is much more than that. It is the story of one who looks upon her American citizenship as a great "spiritual adventure," and who strives to quicken in others a sense of their opportunities and responsibilities as heirs of the new freedom. She pleads for a generous treatment of all those whom oppression and privation send to make their homes in our land. It is only by being faithful to the ideal of human brotherhood expressed in the Declaration of Independence that our nation can realize its true destiny, she warns us.

Mary Antin was recently urged to write a history of the United States for children, that   would give the inner meaning of the facts as well as a clear account of the really significant events.

"I have long had such a work in mind," she wrote, "and I suppose I shall have to do it some day. In the meantime I *talk* history to my children—my little daughter of eight

16

and the Russian cousin who goes to school in the kitchen. Only yesterday at luncheon I told them about our system of representative government, and our potatoes grew cold on our plates, we were all so absorbed."

In all that Mary Antin writes and in all that she says her faith in her country and her zeal for its honor shine out above all else. To the new pilgrims who lived and suffered in other lands before they sought refuge in America, as well as to those who can say quite literally, "Land where my fathers died," she brings this message:

"We must strive to be worthy of our great heritage as American citizens so that we may use wisely and well its wonderful privileges. To be alive in America is to ride on the central current of the river of modern life; and to have a conscious purpose is to hold the rudder that steers the ship of fate."

# I

THE first thing about his American teachers that struck David Rudinsky was the fact that they were women, and the second was that they did not get angry if somebody asked questions. This phenomenon subverted his previous experience. When he went to *heder* (Hebrew school), in Russia, his teachers were always men, and they did not like to be interrupted with questions that were not in the lesson. Everything was different in America, and David liked the difference.

The American teachers, on their part, also made comparisons. They said David was not like other children. It was not merely that his mind worked like lightning; those neglected Russian waifs were almost always quick to learn, perhaps because they had to make up for lost time. The quality of his interest, more than the rapidity of his progress, excited comment. Miss Ralston, David's teacher in the sixth grade, which he reached in his second year at school, said of him that he never let go of a lesson till he had got the soul of the matter. 'I don't think grammar is grammar to him,' she said, 'or fractions mere arithmetic. I'm not satisfied with the way I teach these things since I've had David. I feel that if he were on the platform instead of me, geography and grammar would be spliced to the core of the universe.'

One difficulty David's teachers encountered, and that was his extreme reserve. In private conversation it was hard to get anything out of him except 'yes, ma'am' and 'no, ma'am,' or, 'I don't understand, please.' In the classroom he did not seem to be aware of the existence of anybody besides Teacher and himself. He asked questions as fast as he could formulate them, and Teacher had to exercise much tact in order to satisfy him without slighting the rest of her pupils. To advances of a personal sort he did not respond, as if friendship were not among the things he hungered for.

It was Miss Ralston who found the way to David's heart. Perhaps she was interested in such things; they sometimes are, in the public schools. After the Christmas holidays, the children were given as a subject for composition, 'How I spent the Vacation.' David wrote in a froth of enthusiasm about whole days spent in the public library. He covered twelve pages with an account of the books he had read. The list included many juvenile classics in American history and biography; and from his comments it was plain that the little alien worshiped the heroes of war.

When Miss Ralston had read David's composition, she knew what to do. She was one of those persons who always know what to do, and do it. She asked David to stay after school, and read to him, from a blue book with gilt lettering, 'Paul Revere's Ride' and 'Independence Bell.' That hour neither of them ever forgot. To David it seemed as if all the heroes he had dreamed of crowded around him, so real did his teacher's reading make them. He heard the clash of swords and the flapping of banners in the wind. On the blackboard behind Miss Ralston troops of faces appeared and vanished, like the shadows that run across a hillside when clouds are moving in the sky. As for Miss Ralston, she said afterwards that she was the first person who had ever seen the real David Rudinsky. That was a curious statement to make, considering that his mother and father, and sundry other persons in the two hemispheres, had had some acquaintance with David previous to the reading of 'Paul Revere's Ride.' However, Miss Ralston had a way of saying curious things.

There were many readings out of school hours, after that memorable beginning. Miss Ralston did not seem to realize that the School Board did not pay her for those extra hours that she spent on David. David did not know that she was paid at all. He thought Teacher was born on purpose to read and tell him things and answer his questions, just as his mother existed to cook his favorite soup and patch his trousers. So he brought his pet book from the library, and when the last pupil was gone, he took it from his desk and laid it on Miss Ralston's, without a word; and Miss Ralston read, and they were both happy. When a little Jewish boy from Russia goes to school in America, all sorts of things are likely to happen that the School Board does not provide for. It might be amusing to figure out the reasons.

David's reserve slowly melted in the glowing intimacy of these happy half-hours; still, he seldom made any comment on the reading at the time; he basked mutely in the warmth of his teacher's sympathy. But what he did not say orally he was very likely to say on paper. That also was one of Miss Ralston's discoveries. When she gave out the theme, 'What I Mean to Do When I Grow Up,' David wrote that he was going to be an American citizen, and always vote for honest candidates, and belong to a society for arresting illegal voters. You see David was only a greenhorn, and an excitable one. He thought it a very great matter to be a citizen, perhaps because such a thing was not allowed in the country he came from. Miss Ralston probably knew how it was with him, or she guessed. She was great at guessing, as all her children knew. At any rate, she did not smile as she read of David's patriotic ambitions. She put his paper aside until their next quiet hour, and then she used it so as to get a great deal out of him that he would not have had the courage to tell if he had not believed that it was an exercise in composition.

This Miss Ralston was a crafty person. She learned from David about a Jewish restaurant where his father sometimes took him; a place where a group of ardent young Russians discussed politics over their inexpensive dinner. She heard about a mass meeting of Russian Jews to celebrate the death of Alexander III, 'because he was a cruel tyrant, and was very bad to Jewish people.' She even tracked some astonishing phrases in David's vocabulary to their origin in the Sunday orations he had heard on the Common, in his father's company.

Impressed by these and other signs of paternal interest in her pupil's education, Miss Ralston was not unprepared for the visit which David's father paid her soon after these revelations. It was a very cold day, and Mr. Rudinsky shivered in his thin, shabby overcoat; but his face glowed with inner warmth as he discovered David's undersized figure in one of the front seats.

'I don't know how to say it what I feel to see my boy sitting and learning like this,' he said, with a vibration in his voice that told more than his words. 'Do you know, ma'am, if I didn't have to make a living, I'd like to stay here all day and see my David get educated. I'm forty years old, and I've had much in my life, but it's worth nothing so much as this. The day I brought my children to school, it was the best day in my life. Perhaps you won't believe me, ma'am, but when I hear that David is a good boy and learns good in school, I wouldn't change places with Vanderbilt the millionaire.'

He looked at Miss Ralston with the eyes of David listening to 'Paul Revere's Ride.'

'What do you think, ma'am,' he asked, as he got up to leave, 'my David will be a good American, no?'

'He ought to be,' said Miss Ralston, warmly, 'with such a father.'

Mr. Rudinsky did not try to hide his gratification.

'I am a citizen,' he said, unconsciously straightening. 'I took out citizen papers as soon as I came to America, four years ago.'

So they came to the middle of February, when preparations for Washington's Birthday were well along. One day the class was singing 'America,' when Miss Ralston noticed that David stopped and stared absently at the blackboard in front of him. He did not wake out of his reverie till the singing was over, and then he raised his hand.

'Teacher,' he asked, when he had permission to speak, 'what does it mean, "Land where my fathers died"?'

Miss Ralston explained, wondering how many of her pupils cared to analyze the familiar words as David did.

A few days later, the national hymn was sung again. Miss Ralston watched David. His lips formed the words 'Land where my fathers died,' and then they stopped, set in the pout of childish trouble. His eyes fixed themselves on the teacher's, but her smile of encouragement failed to dispel his evident perplexity.

Anxious to help him over his unaccountable difficulty, Miss Ralston detained him after school.

'David,' she asked him, when they were alone, 'do you understand "America" now?'

'Yes, ma'am.'

'Do you understand "Land where my fathers died"?'

'Yes, ma'am.'

'You didn't sing with the others.'

'No, ma'am.'

Miss Ralston thought of a question that would rouse him.

'Don't you like "America," David?'

The boy almost jumped in his place.

'Oh, yes, ma'am, I do! I like "America." It's—fine.'

He pressed his fist nervously to his mouth, a trick he had when excited.

'Tell me, David, why you don't sing it.'

David's eyes fixed themselves in a look of hopeless longing. He answered in a whisper, his pale face slowly reddening.

'My fathers didn't die here. How can I sing such a lie?'

Miss Ralston's impulse was to hug the child, but she was afraid of startling him. The attention she had lavished on the boy was rewarded at this moment, when her understanding of his nature inspired the answer to his troubled question. She saw how his mind worked. She realized, what a less sympathetic witness might have failed to realize, that behind the moral scruple expressed in his words, there was a sense of irreparable loss derived from the knowledge that he had no share in the national past. The other children could shout the American hymn in all the pride of proprietorship, but to him the words did not apply. It was a flaw in his citizenship, which he was so jealous to establish.

The teacher's words were the very essence of tact and sympathy. In her voice were mingled the yearning of a mother and the faith of a comrade.

'David Rudinsky, you have as much a right to those words as I or anybody else in America. Your ancestors did not die on our battlefields, but they would have if they'd had a chance. You used to spend all your time reading the Hebrew books, in Russia. Don't you know how your people—your ancestors, perhaps!—fought the Roman tyrants? Don't you remember the Maccabean brothers, and Bar Kochba, and—oh, you know about them more than I! I'm ashamed to tell you that I haven't read much Jewish history, but I'm sure if we begin to look it up, we'll find that people of your race—people like your father, David—took part in the fight for freedom, wherever they were allowed. And even in this country—David, I'm going to find out for you how many Jews there were in the armies of the Revolution. We don't think about it here, you see, because we don't ask what a man's religion is, as long as he is brave and good.'

David's eyes slowly lost their look of distress as his teacher talked. His tense little face, upturned to hers, reminded her of a withered blossom that revives in the rain. She went on with increasing earnestness, herself interested in the discoveries she was making, in her need.

'I tell you the truth, David, I never thought of these things before, but I do believe that the Pilgrim Fathers didn't all come here before the Revolution. Isn't your father just like them? Think of it, dear, how he left his home, and came to a strange land, where he couldn't even speak the language. That was a great trouble, you know; something like the fear of the Indians in the old days. And wasn't he looking for the very same things? He wanted freedom for himself and his family, and a chance for his children to grow up wise and brave. You know your father cares more for such things than he does for money or anything. It's the same story over again. Every ship that brings your people from Russia and other countries where they are ill-treated is a Mayflower. If I were a Jewish child like you, I would sing "America" louder than anybody else!'

David's adoring eyes gave her the thanks which his tongue

would not venture to utter. Never since that moment, soon after his arrival from Russia, when his father showed him his citizenship papers, saying, 'Look, my son, this makes you an American,' had he felt so secure in his place in the world.

Miss Ralston studied his face in silence while she gathered up some papers on her desk, preparatory to leaving. In the back of her mind she asked herself to how many of the native children in her class the Fourth of July meant anything besides fire-crackers.

'Get your things, David,' she said presently, as she locked her desk. 'It's time we were going. Think if we should get locked up in the building!'

David smiled absently. In his ears ran the familiar line, 'Land where my fathers died—my fathers died—fathers died.'

'It's something like the Psalms!' he said suddenly, himself surprised at the discovery.

'What is like the Psalms, dear?'

He hesitated. Now that he had to explain, he was not sure any more. Miss Ralston helped him out.

'You mean "America," sounds like the Psalms to you?' David nodded. His teacher beamed her understanding. How did she guess wherein the similarity lay? David had in mind such moments as this when he said of Miss Ralston, 'Teacher talks with her eyes.'

Miss Ralston went to get her coat and hat from the closet.

'Get your things, David,' she repeated. 'The janitor will come to chase us out in a minute.'

He was struggling with the torn lining of a coat-sleeve in the children's dressing-room, when he heard Miss Ralston exclaim,—

'Oh, David! I had almost forgotten. You must try this on. This is what you're going to wear when you speak the dialogue with Annie and Raymond. We used it in a play a few years ago. I thought it would do for you.'

She held up a blue-and-buff jacket with tarnished epaulets. David hurried to put it on. He was to take the part of George Washington in the dialogue. At sight of the costume, his heart started off on a gallop.

Alas for his gallant aspirations! Nothing of David was visible outside the jacket except two big eyes above and two blunt boot-toes below. The collar reached to his ears; the cuffs dangled below his knees. He resembled a scarecrow in the cornfield more than the Father of his Country.

Miss Ralston suppressed her desire to laugh.

'It's a little big, isn't it?' she said cheerily, holding up the shoulders of the heroic garment. 'I wonder how we can make it fit. Don't you think your mother would know how to take up the sleeves and do something to the back?'

She turned the boy around, more hopeless than she would let him see. Miss Ralston understood more about little boys' hearts than about their coats.

'How old are you, David?' she asked, absently, wondering for the hundredth time at his diminutive stature. 'I thought the boy for whom this was made was about your age.'

David's face showed that he felt reproved. 'I'm twelve,' he said, apologetically.

Miss Ralston reproached herself for her tactlessness, and proceeded to make amends.

'Twelve?' she repeated, patting the blue shoulders. 'You speak the lines like a much older boy. I'm sure your mother can make the coat fit, and I'll bring the wig—a powdered wig—and the sword, David! You'll look just like George Washington!'

Her gay voice echoed in the empty room. Her friendly eyes challenged his. She expected to see him kindle, as he did so readily in these days of patriotic excitement. But David failed to respond. He remained motionless in his place, his eyes blank and staring. Miss Ralston had the feeling that behind his dead front his soul was running away from her.

This is just what was happening. David was running away from her, and from himself, and from the image of George Washington, conjured up by the scene with the military coat. Somewhere in the jungle of his consciousness a monster was stirring, and his soul fled in terror of its clutch. What was it—what was it that came tearing through the wilderness of his memories of two worlds? In vain he tried not to understand. The ghosts of forgotten impressions cackled in the wake of the pursuing monster, the breath of whose nostrils spread an odor of evil sophistries grafted on his boyish thoughts in a chimerical past.

His mind reeled in a whirlwind of recollection. Miss Ralston could not have understood some of the things David reviewed, even if he had tried to tell her. In that other life of his, in Russia, had been monstrous things, things that seemed unbelievable to David himself, after his short experience of America. He had suffered many wrongs,—yes, even as a little boy,—but he was not thinking of past grievances as he stood before Miss Ralston, seeing her as one sees a light through a fog. He was thinking of things harder to forget than injuries received from others. It was a sudden sense of his own sins that frightened David, and of one sin in particular, the origin of which was buried somewhere in the slime of the evil past. David was caught in the meshes of a complex inheritance; contradictory impulses tore at his heart. Fearfully he dived to the bottom of his consciousness, and brought up a bitter conviction: David Rudinsky, who called himself an American, who worshiped the names of the heroes, suddenly knew that he had sinned, sinned against his best friend, sinned even as he was planning to impersonate George Washington, the pattern of honor.

His white forehead glistened with the sweat of anguish. His eyes sickened. Miss Ralston caught him as he wavered and put him in the nearest seat.

'Why, David! what's the matter? Are you ill? Let me take this off—it's so heavy. There, that's better. Just rest your head on me, so.'

This roused him. He wriggled away from her support, and put out a hand to keep her off.

'Why, David! what *is* the matter? Your hands are so cold—'

David's head felt heavy and wobbly, but he stood up and began to put on his coat again, which he had pulled off in order to try on the uniform. To Miss Ralston's anxious questions he answered not a syllable, neither did he look at her once. His teacher, thoroughly alarmed, hurriedly put on her street things, intending to take him home. They walked in silence through the empty corridors, down the stairs, and across the school yard. The teacher noticed with relief that the boy grew steadier with every step. She smiled at him encouragingly when he opened the gate for her, as she had taught him, but he did not meet her look.

At the corner where they usually parted David paused, steeling himself to take his teacher's hand; but to his surprise she kept right on, taking *his* crossing.

It was now that he spoke, and Miss Ralston was astonished at the alarm in his voice.

'Miss Ralston, where are you going? You don't go this way.'

'I'm going to see you home, David,' she replied firmly. 'I can't let you go alone—like this.'

'Oh, teacher, don't, please don't! I'm all right—I'm not sick,—it's not far—Don't, Miss Ralston, *please*!'

In the February dusk, Miss Ralston saw the tears rise to his eyes. Whatever was wrong with him, it was plain that her presence only made him suffer the more. Accordingly she yielded to his entreaty.

'I hope you'll be all right, David,' she said, in a tone she might have used to a full-grown man. 'Good-bye.' And she turned the corner.

## II

All the way home Miss Ralston debated the wisdom of allowing him to go alone, but as she recalled his look and his entreating voice, she felt anew the compulsion that had made her yield. She attributed his sudden breakdown entirely to overwrought nerves, and remorsefully resolved not to subject him in the future to the strain of extra hours after school.

Her misgivings were revived the next morning, when David failed to appear with the ringing of the first gong, as was his habit. But before the children had taken their seats, David's younger brother, Bennie, brought her news of the missing boy.

'David's sick in bed,' he announced in accents of extreme importance. 'He didn't come home till awful late last night, and he was so frozen, his teeth knocked together. My mother says he burned like a fire all night, and she had to take little Harry in her bed, with her and papa, so's David could sleep all alone. We all went downstairs in our bare feet this morning, and dressed ourselves in the kitchen, so David could sleep.'

'What is the matter with him? Did you have the doctor?'

'No, ma'am, not yet. The dispensary don't open till nine o'clock.'

Miss Ralston begged him to report again in the afternoon, which he did, standing before her, cap in hand, his sense of importance still dominating over brotherly concern.

'He's sick, all right,' Bennie reported. 'He don't eat at all—just drinks and drinks. My mother says he cried the whole morning, when he woke up and found out he'd missed school. My mother says he tried to get up and dress himself, but he couldn't anyhow. Too sick.'

'Did you have the doctor?' interrupted Miss Ralston,

suppressing her impatience.

'No, ma'am, not yet. My father went to the dispensary but the doctor said he can't come till noon, but he didn't. Then I went to the dispensary, dinner time, but the doctor didn't yet come when we went back to school. My mother says you can die ten times before the dispensary doctor comes.'

'What does your mother think it is?'

'Oh, she says it's a bad cold; but David isn't strong, you know, so she's scared. I guess if he gets worse I'll have to stay home from school to run for the medicines.'

'I hope not Bennie. Now you'd better run along, or you'll be late.'

'Yes, ma'am. Good-bye.'

'Will you come again in the morning and tell me about your brother?'

'Yes, ma'am. Good-bye.—Teacher.'

'Yes, Bennie?'

'Do you think you can do something—something—about his *record*? David feels dreadful because he's broke his record. He never missed school before, you know. It's—it's too bad to see him cry. He's always so quiet, you know, kind of like grown people. He don't fight or tease or anything. Do you think you can, teacher?'

Miss Ralston was touched by this tribute to her pupil, but she could not promise to mend the broken record.

'Tell David not to worry. He has the best record in the school, for attendance and everything. Tell him I said he must hurry and get well, as we must rehearse our pieces for Washington's Birthday.'

The next morning Bennie reeled off a longer story than ever. He described the doctor's visit in great detail, and Miss Ralston was relieved to gather that David's ailment was nothing worse than grippe; unless, as the doctor warned, his run-down condition caused complications. He would be in bed a week or more, in any case, 'and he ought to sleep most of the time, the doctor said.'

'I guess the doctor don't know our David!' Bennie scoffed. 'He never wants at all to go to sleep. He reads and reads when everybody goes to bed. One time he was reading all night, and the lamp went out, and he was afraid to go downstairs for oil, because he'd wake somebody, so he lighted matches and read little bits. There was a heap of burned matches in the morning.'

'Dear me!' exclaimed Miss Ralston. 'He ought not to do that. Your father ought not—Does your father allow him to stay up nights?'

'Sure. My father's proud because he's going to be a great man; a doctor, maybe.' He shrugged his shoulders, as if to say, 'What may not a David become?'

'David is funny, don't you think, teacher?' the boy went on. 'He asks such funny questions. What do you think he said to the doctor?'

'I can't imagine.'

'Well, he pulled him by the sleeve when he took out the—the thing he puts in your mouth, and said kind of hoarse, "Doctor, did you ever tell a lie?" Wasn't that funny?'

Miss Ralston did not answer. She was thinking that David must have been turning over some problem in his mind, to say so much to a stranger.

'Did you give him my message?' she asked finally.

'Yes'm! I told him about rehearsing his piece for Washington's Birthday.' Bennie paused.

'Well?'

'He acted so funny. He turned over to the wall, and cried and cried without any noise.'

'The poor boy! He'll be dreadfully disappointed not to take his part in the exercises.'

Bennie shook his head.

'That isn't for what he cries,' he said oracularly.

Miss Ralston's attentive silence invited further revelations.

'He's *worrying* about something,' Bennie brought out, rolling his head ominously.

31

'Why? How do you know?'

'The doctor said so. He told my father downstairs. He said, "Make him tell, if you can, it may help to pull him off"—no, "pull him up." That's what the doctor said.'

Miss Ralston's thoughts flew back to her last interview with David, two days before, when he had broken down so suddenly. Was there a mystery there? She was certain the boy was overwrought, and physically run down. Apparently, also, he had been exposed to the weather during the evening when he was taken ill; Bennie's chatter indicated that David had wandered in the streets for hours. These things would account for the grippe, and for the abnormal fever of which Bennie boasted. But what was David worrying about? She resolved to go and see the boy in a day or two, when he was reported to be more comfortable.

On his next visit Bennie brought a message from the patient himself.

'He said to give you this, teacher,' handing Miss Ralston a journal. 'It's yours. It has the pieces in it for Washington's Birthday. He said you might need it, and the doctor didn't say when he could go again to school.'

Miss Ralston laid the journal carelessly on a pile of other papers. Bennie balanced himself on one foot, looking as if his mission were not yet ended.

'Well, Bennie?' Miss Ralston encouraged him. She was beginning to understand his mysterious airs.

'David was awful careful about that book,' the messenger said impressively. 'He said over and over not to lose it, and not to give it to nobody only you.'

# III

It was not till the end of the day that Miss Ralston took up the journal Bennie had brought. She turned the leaves absently, thinking of David. He would be so disappointed to miss the exercises! And to whom should she give the part of George Washington in the dialogue? She found the piece in the journal. A scrap of paper marked the place. A folded paper. Folded several times. Miss Ralston opened out the paper and found some writing.

'DEAR TEACHER MISS RALSTON,—

'I can't be George Washington any more because I have lied to you. I must not tell you about what, because you would blame somebody who didn't do wrong.

'Your friend,
'DAVID RUDINSKY.'

Again and again Miss Ralston read the note, unable to understand it. David, her David, whose soul was a mirror for every noble idea, had lied to her! What could he mean? What had impelled him? *Somebody who didn't do wrong.* So it was not David alone; there was some complication with another person. She studied the note word for word  and her eyes slowly filled with tears. If the boy had really lied—if the whole thing were not a chimera of his fevered nights—then what must he have suffered of remorse and shame! Her heart went out to him even while her brain was busy with the mystery.

33

She made a swift resolution. She would go to David at once. She was sure he would tell her more than he had written, and it would relieve his mind. She did not dread the possible disclosures. Her knowledge of the boy made her certain that she would find nothing ignoble at the bottom of his mystery. He was only a child, after all—an overwrought, sensitive child. No doubt he exaggerated his sin, if sin there were. It was her duty to go and put him at rest.

She knew that David's father kept a candy shop in the basement of his tenement, and she had no trouble in finding the place. Half the children in the neighborhood escorted her to the door, attracted by the phenomenon of a teacher loose on their streets.

The tinkle of the shop-bell brought Mr. Rudinsky from the little kitchen in the rear.

'Well, well!' he exclaimed, shaking hands heartily. 'This is a great honor—a great honor.' He sounded the initial  h.  'I wish I had a palace for you to come in, ma'am. I don't think there was such company in this house since it was built.'

His tone was one of genuine gratification. Ushering her into the kitchen, he set a chair for her, and himself sat down at a respectful distance.

'I'm sorry,' he began, with a wave of his hand around the room. 'Such company ought not to sit in the kitchen, but you see—'

He was interrupted by Bennie, who had clattered in at the visitor's heels, panting for recognition.

'Never mind, teacher,' the youngster spoke up, 'we got a parlor upstairs, with a mantelpiece and everything, but David sleeps up there—the doctor said it's the most air—and you dassn't wake him up till he wakes himself.'

Bennie's father frowned, but the visitor smiled a cordial smile.

'I like a friendly kitchen like this,' she said quietly. 'My mother did not keep any help when I was a little girl and I was a great deal in the kitchen.'

Her host showed his appreciation of her tact by dropping the subject.

'I'm sure you came about David,' he said.

'I did. How is he?'

'Pretty sick, ma'am. The doctor says it's not the sickness so much, but David is so weak and small. He says David studies too much altogether. Maybe he's right. What do you think, ma'am?'

Miss Ralston answered remorsefully.

'I agree with the doctor. I think we are all to blame. We push him too much when we ought to hold him back.'

Here Bennie made another raid on the conversation.

'He's going to be a great man, a doctor maybe. My mother says—'

Mr. Rudinsky did not let him finish. He thought it time to insure the peace of so important an interview.

'Bennie,' said he, 'you will go mind the store, and keep the kitchen door shut.'

Bennie's discomfiture was evident in his face. He obeyed, but not without a murmur.

'Let us make a covenant to take better care of David in the future.'

Miss Ralston was speaking when Mrs. Rudinsky appeared in the doorway. She was flushed from the exertions of a hasty toilet, for which she had fled upstairs at theapproach of 'company.' She came forward timidly, holding out a hand on which the scrubbing brush and the paring knife had left their respective marks.

'How do you do, ma'am?' she said, cordially, but shyly. 'I'm glad to see you. I wish I can speak English better, I'd like to say how proud I am to see David's teacher in my house.'

'Why, you speak wonderfully!' Miss Ralston exclaimed, with genuine enthusiasm. 'I don't understand how you pick up the language in such a short time. I couldn't learn Russian so fast, I'm sure.'

'My husband makes us speak English all the time,' Mrs. Rudinsky replied. 'From the fust day he said to speak English. He scolds the children if he hears they speak Jewish.'

'Sure,' put in her husband, 'I don't want my family to be greenhorns.'

Miss Ralston turned a glowing face to him.

'Mr. Rudinsky, I think you've done wonders for your family. If all immigrants were like you, we wouldn't need any restriction laws.' She threw all possible emphasis into her cordial voice. 'Why, you're a better American than some natives I know!'

Mrs. Rudinsky sent her husband a look of loving pride.

'He wants to be a Yankee,' she said.

Her husband took up the cue in earnest.

'Yes, ma'am,' he said, 'that's my ambition. When I was a young man, in the old country, I wanted to be a scholar. But a Jew has no chance in the old country; perhaps you know how it is. It wasn't the Hebrew books I wanted. I wanted to learn what the rest of the world learned, but a poor Jew had no chance in Russia. When I got to America, it was too late for me to go to school. It took me all my time and strength to make a living—I've never been much good in business, ma'am—and when I got my family over, I saw that it was the children would go to school for me. I'm glad to be a plain citizen, if my children will be educated Americans.'

People with eyes and hands like Mr. Rudinsky's can say a great deal in a few words. Miss Ralston felt as if she had known him all his life, and followed his strivings in two worlds.

'I'm glad to know you, Mr. Rudinsky,' she said in a low voice. 'I wish more of my pupils had fathers like David's.'

Her host changed the subject very neatly.

'And I wish the school children had more teachers like you. David likes you so much.'

'Oh, he liked you!' the wife confirmed. 'Please stay till he veks up. He'll be sorry to missed your vis*it*.'

While his wife moved quietly around the stove, making tea, Mr. Rudinsky entertained their guest with anecdotes of David's Hebrew-school days, and of his vain efforts to get at secular books.

'He was just like me,' he said. 'He wanted to learn everything.

36

I couldn't afford a private teacher, and they wouldn't take him in the public school. He learned Russian all alone, and if he got a book from somewhere—a history or anything—he wouldn't eat or drink till he read it all.'

Mrs. Rudinsky often glanced at David's teacher, to see how her husband's stories were impressing her. She was too shy with her English to say more than was required of her as hostess, but her face, aglow with motherly pride, showed how she participated in her husband's enthusiasm.

'You see yourself, ma'am, what he is,' said David's father, 'but what could I make of him in Russia? I was happy when he got here, only it was a little late. I wished he started in school younger.'

'He has time enough,' said Miss Ralston. 'He'll get through grammar school before he's fourteen. He's twelve now, isn't he?'

'Yes, ma'am—no, ma'am! He's really fourteen now, but I made him out younger on purpose.'

Miss Ralston looked puzzled. Mr. Rudinsky explained.

'You see, ma'am, he was twelve years when he came, and I wanted he should go to school as long as possible, so when I made his school certificate, I said he was only ten. I have seven children, and David is the oldest one, and I was afraid he'd have to go to work, if business was bad, or if I was sick. The state is a good father to the children in America, if the real fathers don't mix in. Why should my David lose his chance to get educated and be somebody, because I am a poor business man, and have too many children? So I made out that he had to go to school two years more.'

He narrated this anecdote in the same simple manner in which he had told a dozen others. He seemed pleased to rehearse the little plot whereby he had insured his boy's education. As Miss Ralston did not make any comment immediately, he went on, as if sure of her sympathy.

'I told you I got my citizen papers right away when I came to America. I worked hard before I could bring my family—it took me four years to save the money—and they found a very poor home when they got here, but they were citizens right away. But it wouldn't do them much good, if they didn't get educated. I found out all about the compulsory education, and I said to myself that's the policeman that will keep me from robbing my David if I fail in business.'

He did not overestimate his visitor's sympathy. Miss Ralston followed his story with quick appreciation of his ideals and motives, but in her ingenuous American mind one fact separated itself from the others: namely, that Mr. Rudinsky had falsified his boy's age, and had recorded the falsehood in a public document. Her recognition of the fact carried with it no criticism. She realized that Mr. Rudinsky's conscience was the product of an environment vastly different from hers. It was merely that to her mind the element of deceit was something to be accounted for, be it ever so charitably, whereas in Mr. Rudinsky's mind it evidently had no existence at all.

'So David is really fourteen years old?' she repeated incredulously. 'Why, he seems too little even for twelve! Does he know?—Of course he would know! I wonder that he consented—'

She broke off, struck by a sudden thought. 'Consented to tell a lie' she had meant to say, but the unspoken words diverted her mind from the conversation. It came upon her in a flash that she had found the key to David's mystery. His note was in her pocketbook, but she knew every word of it, and now everything was plain to her. The lie was this lie about his age, and the person he wanted to shield was his father. And for that he was suffering so!

She began to ask questions eagerly.

'Has David said anything about—about a little trouble he had in school the day he became ill?'

Both parents showed concern.

'Trouble? what trouble?'

'Oh, it was hardly trouble—at least, I couldn't tell myself.'

'David is so hard to understand sometimes,' his father said.

'Oh, I don't think so!' the teacher cried. 'Not when you make friends with him. He doesn't say much, it's true, but his heart is like a crystal.'

'He's too still,' the mother insisted, shaking her head. 'All the time he's sick, he don't say anything, only when we ask him something. The doctor thinks he's worrying about something, but he don't tell.'

The mother sighed, but Miss Ralston cut short her reflections.

'Mrs. Rudinsky—Mr. Rudinsky,' she began eagerly, '*I* can tell you what David's troubled about.'

And she told them the story of her last talk with David, and finally read them his note.

'And this lie,' she ended, 'you know what it is, don't you? You've just told me yourself, Mr. Rudinsky.'

She looked pleadingly at him, longing to have him understand David's mind as she understood it. But Mr. Rudinsky was very slow to grasp the point.

'You mean—about the certificate? Because I made out that he was younger?'

Miss Ralston nodded.

'You know David has such a sense of honor,' she explained, speaking slowly, embarrassed by the effort of following Mr. Rudinsky's train of thought and her own at the same time. 'You know how he questions everything—sooner or later he makes everything clear to himself—and something must have started him thinking of this old matter lately—Why, of course! I remember I asked him his age that day, when he tried on the costume, and he answered as usual, and then, I suppose, he suddenly*realized*  what he was saying. I don't believe he ever *thought* about it since—since you arranged it so, and now, all of a sudden—'

She did not finish, because she saw that her listeners did not follow her. Both their faces expressed pain and perplexity. After a long silence, David's father spoke.

'And what do *you* think, ma'am?'

Miss Ralston was touched by the undertone of submission in his voice. Her swift sympathy had taken her far into his thoughts. She recognized in his story one of those ethical paradoxes which the helpless Jews of the Pale, in their search for a weapon that their oppressors could not confiscate, have evolved for their self-defence. She knew that to many honest Jewish minds a lie was not a lie when told to an official; and she divined that no ghost of a scruple had disturbed Mr. Rudinsky in his sense of triumph over circumstances, when he invented the lie that was to insure the education of his gifted child. With David, of course, the same philosophy had been valid. His father's plan for the protection of his future, hingeing on a too familiar sophistry, had dropped innocuous into his consciousness, until, in a moment of spiritual sensitiveness, it took on the visage of sin.

'And what do *you* think, ma'am?'

David's father did not have to wait a moment for her answer, so readily did her insight come to his defense. In a few eager sentences she made him feel that she understood perfectly, and understood David perfectly.

'I respect you the more for that lie, Mr. Rudinsky. It was—a *noble* lie!' There was the least tremor in her voice. 'And I love David for the way *he* sees it.'

Mr. Rudinsky got up and paced slowly across the room. Then he stopped before Miss Ralston.

'You are very kind to talk like that, Miss Ralston,' he said, with peculiar dignity. 'You see the whole thing. In the old country we had to do such things so many times that we—got used to them. Here—here we don't have to.' His voice took on a musing quality. 'But we don't see it right away when we get here. I meant nothing, only just to keep my boy in school. It was not to cheat anybody. The state is willing to educate the children. I said to myself I will tie my own hands, so that I can't pull mychild after me if I drown. I did want my David should have the best chance in America.'

Miss Ralston was thrilled by the suppressed passion in his

voice. She held out her hand to him, saying again, in the low tones that come from the heart, 'I am glad I know you, Mr. Rudinsky.'

There was unconscious chivalry in Mr. Rudinsky's next words. Stepping to his wife's side, he laid a gentle hand on her shoulder, and said quietly, 'My wife has been my helper in everything.'

Miss Ralston, as we know, was given to seeing things. She saw now, not a poor immigrant couple in the first stage of American respectability, which was all there was in the room to see, but a phantom procession of men with the faces of prophets, muffled in striped praying-shawls, and women radiant in the light of many candles, and youths and maidens with smouldering depths in their eyes, and silent children who pushed away joyous things for—for—

Dreams don't use up much time. Mr. Rudinsky was not aware that there had been a pause before he spoke again.

'You understand so well, Miss Ralston. But David'—he hesitated a moment, then finished quickly. 'How can he respect me if he feels like that?'

His wife spoke tremulously from her corner.

'That's what I think.'

'Oh, don't think that!' Miss Ralston cried. 'He does respect you—he understands. Don't you see what he says: *I can't tell you—because you would blame somebody who didn't do wrong.* He doesn't blame you. He only blames himself. He's afraid to tell me because he thinks *I* can't understand.'

The teacher laughed a happy little laugh. In her eagerness to comfort David's parents, she said just the right things, and every word summed up an instantaneous discovery. One of her useful gifts was the ability to find out truths just when she desperately needed them. There are people like that, and some of them are school-teachers hired by the year. When David's father cried, 'How can he respect me?' Miss Ralston's heart was frightened while it beat one beat. Only one. Then she knew all David's thoughts between the terrible, 'I have lied,' and the generous, 'But my father did no wrong.' She guessed what the struggle had cost to reconcile the contradictions; she imagined his bewilderment as he tried to rule himself by his new-found standards, while seeking excuses for his father in the one he cast away from him as unworthy of an American. Problems like David's are not very common, but then Miss Ralston was good at guessing.

'Don't worry, Mr. Rudinsky,' she said, looking out of her glad eyes. 'And you, Mrs. Rudinsky, don't think for a moment that David doesn't understand. He's had a bad time, the poor boy, but I know—Oh, I must speak to him! Will he wake soon, do you think?'

Mr. Rudinsky left the room without a word.

'It's all right,' said David's mother, in reply to an anxious look from Miss Ralston. 'He sleeps already the whole afternoon.'

It had grown almost dark while they talked. Mrs. Rudinsky now lighted the lamps, apologizing to her guest for not having done so sooner, and then she released Bennie from his prolonged attendance in the store.

Bennie came into the kitchen chewing his reward, some very gummy confection. He was obliged to look the pent-up things he wanted to say, until such time as he could clear his clogged talking-gear.

'Teacher,' he began, before he had finished swallowing, 'What for did you say—'

'Bennie!' his mother reproved him, 'You must shame yourself to listen by the door.'

'Well, there wasn't any trade, ma,' he defended himself, 'only Bessie Katz, and she brought back the peppermints she bought this morning, to change them for taffy, but I didn't because they were all dirty, and one was broken—'

Bennie never had a chance to bring his speeches to a voluntary stop: somebody always interrupted. This time it was his father, who came down the stairs, looking so grave that even Bennie was impressed.

'He's awake,' said Mr. Rudinsky. 'I lighted the lamp. Will you please come up, ma'am?'

He showed her to the room where David lay, and closed the door on them both. It was not he, but Miss Ralston, the American teacher, that his boy needed. He went softly down to the kitchen, where his wife smiled at him through unnecessary tears.

Miss Ralston never forgot the next hour, and David never forgot. The woman always remembered how the boy's eyes burned through the dusk of the shadowed corner where he lay. The boy remembered how his teacher's voice palpitated in his heart, how her cool hands rested on his, how the lamplight made a halo out of her hair. To each of them the dim room with its scant furnishings became a spiritual rendezvous.

What did the woman say, that drew the sting of remorse from the child's heart, without robbing him of the bloom of his idealism? What did she tell him that transmuted the offense of ages into the marrow and blood of persecuted virtue? How did she weld in the boy's consciousness the scraps of his mixed inheritance, so that he saw his whole experience as an unbroken thing at last? There was nobody to report how it was done. The woman did not know nor the child. It was a secret born of the boy's need and the woman's longing to serve him; just as in nature every want creates its satisfaction.

When she was ready to leave him, Miss Ralston knelt for a moment at David's bedside, and once more took his small hot hands in hers.

'And I have made a discovery, David,' she said, smiling in a way of her own. 'Talking with your parents downstairs I saw why it was that the Russian Jews are so soon at home here in our dear country. In the hearts of men like your father, dear, is the true America.'